UNICORN DREAMS

BY DYAN SHELDON

ILLUSTRATED BY NEIL REED

Dial Books for Young Readers

NEW YORK

The first time Dan saw the unicorn, he was staring out the window of his classroom watching the traffic. He saw a long silvery tail, braided with a red ribbon, vanish behind a bus.

Dan's teacher tapped her ruler on her desk. "Dan," she said. "Dan, are you daydreaming again?"

Dan looked up. "No, ma'am," he said.

Dan's teacher smiled. "Then perhaps you'd like to tell the class what you were looking at that was more interesting than our lesson."

Dan pointed to the window. "There's a unicorn outside," he told her.

Dan's teacher didn't look out the window. "A unicorn? You saw a unicorn in front of the school?"

"That's right," said Dan, nodding with excitement. "It had a long silvery tail, tied with a red ribbon."

The other children began to laugh. "Dreamy Dan!" they shouted. "He sees unicorns on Maple Street."

Dan bent his head over his math problems.

The second time he saw the unicorn, Dan was on the school bus, taking a trip with his class.

The unicorn was gazing at the road from the window of the video store. It shook its head when it saw Dan.

Dan waved back.

Dan's teacher appeared at his shoulder. "Who are you waving to, Dan?" she asked.

"The unicorn," cried Dan, pointing toward the video store. "It shook its head at me."

Dan's teacher didn't look back at the video store. She squeezed her lips together. "The unicorn," she repeated. "The unicorn was in the video store?"

"Dreamy Dan! Dreamy Dan!" chanted the other children. "He thinks unicorns go shopping on Main Street."

Even the bus driver started to laugh.

The third time Dan saw the unicorn, he was in the school yard. The other children were playing games, and the unicorn was under a tree, eating an apple it had found in the trash. When it saw Dan, the unicorn threw the apple in the air and caught it on its horn.

Dan's teacher blew her whistle. "Dan!" she called. "Why aren't you playing with everyone else? What are you doing?"

"I'm watching the unicorn," Dan called back. He raised his hand. "It's over there."

Dan's teacher didn't turn around. "A unicorn in the playground?" she said.

"That's right!" cried Dan. "It's juggling an apple."

The other children had stopped their games and were all watching Dan.

"Dreamy Dan! Dreamy Dan!" they teased. "He thinks unicorns are real."

Dan's teacher blew her whistle again, but no one heard it because they were laughing so hard.

When Dan got home from school that afternoon, the unicorn was lying in the grass in front of Dan's building. It stood up when it saw Dan.

The bells on its mane jangled as it followed him into the elevator. "You can't come in," said Dan. But the unicorn went in anyway.

Dan and the unicorn got out on the fourteenth floor. "You can't come in," Dan told the unicorn as he opened the door to his apartment. "Everyone says that you aren't real." But the unicorn went in anyway.

All afternoon Dan waited for the unicorn to vanish, but instead it followed him everywhere he went.

It shared his snack.

It helped him with his homework.

It watched television with him.

When Dan went to bed, the unicorn went too.
They had wonderful dreams.

The next day the unicorn walked to school with Dan.

When Dan went to school on his own, he walked through ordinary streets, past ordinary buildings.

But with the unicorn he walked through an enchanted forest where dragons played and wizards worked spells.

They had just come to the edge of the forest when the school bell rang.

Dan was saying good-bye
to the unicorn when his
teacher called him in. Dan
ran toward the school.

"Come on, Dreamy Dan!"
yelled a boy from his class.

"Where's your unicorn?"
teased another.

Dan looked back. The
unicorn was gone.

Dan spent the morning
staring out the window at
the dull, gray street. He
missed the unicorn.

In the afternoon it was story time. "Would anyone like to tell a story today?" asked the teacher.

Suddenly Dan's eyes lit up and he raised his hand.

Everyone listened as Dan told the class how the unicorn had followed him into the elevator. He told them how the bells on its mane jangled and how butterflies danced in the air all around it.

He told them about his wonderful dreams with the unicorn.

This time no one laughed.

"I can hear them!" shouted one of the children. "I can hear the bells!"

"Look!" cried another. "Look over there."

Now all the children could see Dan's unicorn. It stood at the top of a narrow path, leading to green fields below. It looked at Dan and flicked its tail.

Dan followed the unicorn . . . and the rest of the class followed Dan.

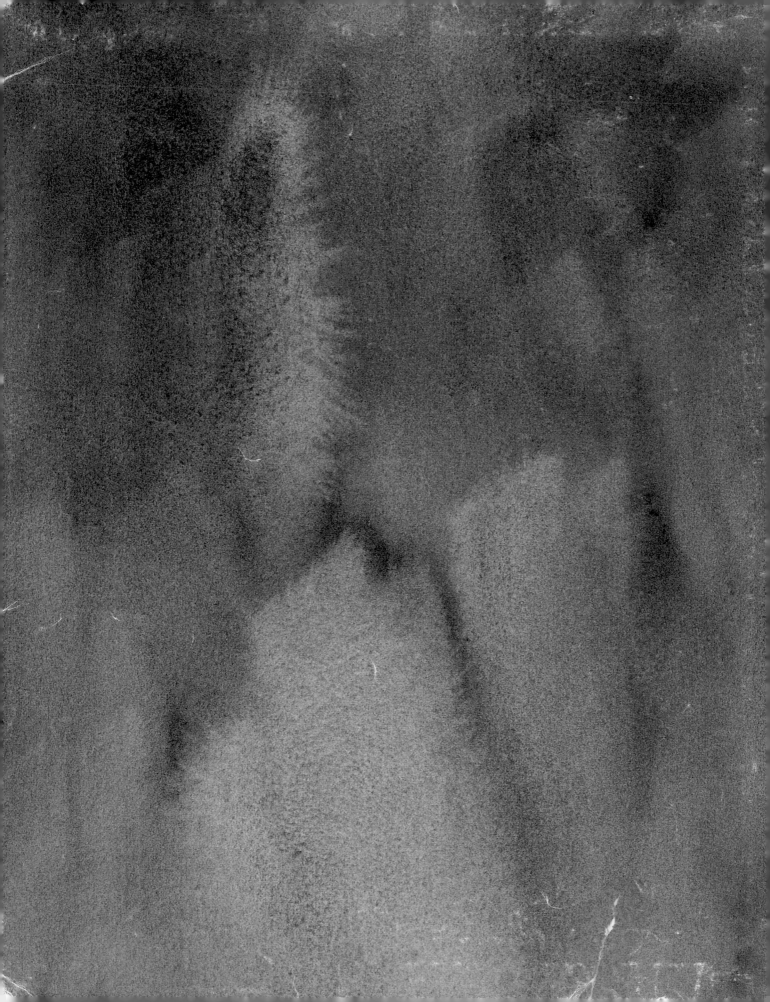